A RACE AGAINST DEATH

From Alicia x

This book contains discussions of murder, death and assault. Discretion is advised.

Copyright © 2024 Alicia Lloyd

All rights reserved. No part of this book may be reproduced or used in any manner without the prior written permission of the copyright owner, except for the use of brief quotations in a book review.

Paperback: 979-8325602757

First paperback edition June 2024
This paperback edition September 2024

Editing by Faith Fawcett

'A gripping approach to the murder mystery genre' - Sophie, Amazon Reviewer

'There is a real sense of talent here and I've never read anything like this before' - Faith Fawcett, author of *Lost For You*

'Lloyd's writing is sharp, her pacing relentless' - Steve, Amazon Reviewer

Prologue

A sudden jolt in the car.
A mist of wings and fury driving the force.
An illusion of blood dripping down the wall.
But is it an illusion,
Is it real?
Is it a fictional piece of man-made steel?

A person lays below the car,
Frayed, dishevelled,
Looking up, closed-eyed, to the dark dim sky.
A person walks by to see a figure, cold and dead,
Stab wounds in the head,
Who could have done it?
Who was the victim?
Who, what, where and why?

Carla

I am walking down the road.
Things seem sinister
But don't they always when alone on the streets at night.
A wave of anxiety hits me like a storm.
For a moment in time, I knew something was wrong.
Something terrible was about to happen.
I knew it,
I knew the feeling well:
The swelling pain in my wrists,
Pounding in my fists,
Wakes me up with a sudden bang,
Crown menace of mind-forged manacles that tempt my ears.
That was, until it ended.

A silver dagger ripped through my skin from behind,
Spilling my blood,
Enraging my face.
I collapse to the floor.
Blood drips on my shoulder.
I knew how this would sadly end.

Death.

A sinister motive.
They betrayed me,
They betrayed me,

They betrayed me.
But I'll never know why.
All I know is that the shadow that lingered behind my shoulder was a friend.
I just don't understand;
What was their game?

My mind races against death,
Trying to hold onto my life just a little longer,
Just a little bit longer.
But as my body jolts forward to the floor,
I know it's the end.

Goodbye.

Harrison

I wake up to the news channel blurring my eyes.
My face goes pale,
My eyelids twitch,
Bones fragments itch,
My glitching body waiting to return.
A body was found.

Could it be *her*?
Oh it couldn't.
It shouldn't be,
Not *her*.

It looks like her
So I shudder.
I'm suddenly so achy,
So numb.
Then they speak and say,
'The body has been identified as Carla Davey.'

Trapped in my own damp skin,
No beauty within,
Pure deception at its finest.
Who did this?

I crumble inside,
Murder on my mind.
I hate and detest the day
As it is left in dismay.

I can't believe she's gone.

Dead as a doornail.
Throat not slit but her stomach punctured.
As she lays below a car,
Dead, and seemingly run over as the blood splatters out of her guts,
Staining the floor and pavement for people to stare at as they walk by,
Something to give out in a rageful sigh.
Gone by the wind,
Gone by the storm.
Never warned;
Just a single pretence and reward.

I'm not who I was a couple minutes ago;
I am a changed man,
Just a lonely heartbreaker of my own self
As I linger through a shroud of doubt in myself.
I was drunk that night.
I remember nothing.
Nothing at all.
I was apart from my body,
Away from the air,
Dynamite clenching my fists like a rumour of sadness.
Could I have done this?
Is there a chance I-
No, not at all.
Unless the manacles I dare see fit tell me otherwise.

I shall see.

Fletcher

I don't remember the part when I found out she died;
It's all such a blur.
I lie, a telling one.
Could the nature I seek be the truth?
When all I see is piles of clues and false confessions
until I look into myself:
A traitor,
A liar.
No, I did no wrong;
I'm good,
A stand up guy
And Carla was…

She was beautiful,
A golden shimmer in the dark,
A wonderful experience,
A good person.
Who would care to kill her?
I have no idea.

Something inside tells me this is more sinister than it seems,
The bloody and frail body tells me so.
Not that it was a murder
But who did it?
Was she stabbed in the back in more ways than one?

I guess I'd better watch *my* back,

I may provoke them to do bad;
Kill me,
I dare you.
Because I'll stand no nonsense.

How could they?
How could they?
How could they?

Not pretty but still death lies like a pain in my backside.
Who chose this, who wanted this?
It's heinous,
It's criminal,
It's beyond mankind's imagination.
It makes me mad,
Cracks the surface of my scalp,
Leaving it to bleed and dry in the chapters between my hair.
I now walk around in madness.

I miss her the more I look in the mirror,
I miss her more than the world could ever tell,
I miss her and would fight for her whilst the world was on fire.
But I can't anymore;
She's gone for good.

I think I know who did this.

Duffy

All I hear now as I go to sleep is screaming,
Constantly,
Just the echo of death in my ear as I wake up in a sudden jolt,
Screaming to myself
Until my lungs burn out and give in;
It can't hold the immense pain I feel.

Oh Carla,
Oh Carla,
Oh Carla!
How could you leave us?
How could they take you?
Who is such a coward?

I suspect who but I shan't say,
Not yet anyway.
The cracks on my skin show enough as it is;
Connect the dots and you'll see.
As I lean into me,
Rigorously singing her praises, I look back at our time together,
Laughing, smiling.
She was pretty tough
But most can't survive such a horrific attack;
It's too hard.
Now I am pulled out of her arms,
Falling apart.

I too thought I might die as I saw the black figure
reach for my throat and choke me.
I grip his hand, trying to pull him away from me
But it doesn't work;
I'm too far gone.
Everything becomes dizzy.
I feel faint but more than that;
The damage has been done,
Dead.

Then I wake up,
Looking beside me for blood or signs of a struggle.
Nothing.

"Drama queen," they call me;
I still think I'd rather be safe than sorry,
With angst more than the sun,
Driven by a blood moon splattered with guilt
Because my hair is wet from sobbing.
As I look up,
The sky erupts in flames;
Fire will fight.
I never feared the verse of hell.

I will beat this killer,
Make them pay
Whatever it takes.

Harrison

I look upon my works,
Trying to remember what I truly did that night Carla died.

Am I a monster?
I was heavily intoxicated;
Would I truly be fully to blame?

Guilt rushed over me like an ocean wave;
Savage,
Ugly.
My own touch now scared me,
Not tempting but it is afraid.
Then I realise;
Surely, if I did it,
There would be clues?

I look around my barren apartment,
Once one of peace.

I find a half-eaten chocolate bar and a box of no remains,
Until I hear a cluttering sound in the washing machine.
In it,
A knife covered in blood,
Damning evidence to me.
But I suppose it could have been planted there,

Yes!
Framed, I say,
Framed,
Right?

I toss the knife in the dishwasher to wash my sins away.
Then I hear
A sound
Knocking at the door.
Who could it be?
Who do I see?
To my surprise Fletcher and Duffy,
Both facing me with perturbed faces.
But at the same time certain that
They'd figured it out, hadn't they?
That I had killed Carla.

I mean, if I did, I didn't mean to,
I didn't intend.
Watch me as I burn and they say,
"Hello Harrison."

I've been caught.

Fletcher

Thunder rips through my skin and lightning deep into my tissue.
I wallow in sadness;
Harrison did it,
I am certain.
He was drunk,
He was an idiot,
After all.
Before the murder, I was there,
The sober driver for him and his mates.
Violence had eaten him alive;
He was slamming doors,
Punching through windows,
He shattered the glass.
For all I know he shattered Carla's skin,
Shattered my brain
Because Carla was dear to me.

What can I do to bring her back?
Back to me, to her family?
Underneath, the stars align; I can see a spelling on Harrison, peering down,
And, above the stars, the underlined word
"murderer."

He did it, didn't he?
He killed Carla.
He killed her,

He *killed* her!

But beside the road I walk on is Duffy,
An old friend of Carla's,
One of the suspects looking rather suspicious,
Ridiculous manners.
I approach her but she ignores me
Till I make her:
'Talk now or else!'
I commanded her.
Scared to death she responded,
'I suppose.'

I turn to look at the pavement,
Then back.
Mistakes part of a hand,
A band,
Tortured and grand,
I grab her wrist and let go;
I don't know why it bothered her so much.
It was an empty promise.

'Harrison did it.'
Paused.
'Did what?'
Paused.
'He killed her, he killed Carla.'

Duffy

A strange man approached me,
Grabbed my wrist,
Then let go.
He threatened me,
Called me names.
I was scared,
I couldn't breathe,
I was alone.

He said, 'Harrison did it.'
He couldn't have.
He shouldn't have.
He wouldn't have.
Surely? Right?

I mean, *Fletcher* is the one who threatened me.
Fletcher is the one who hid me from public view.
It was Fletcher's opinion.
Sounds suspicious to me.

Is Fletcher the murderer?

It all makes sense now;
Fletcher was so defensive,
So forceful,
A dreadful ego.
He did this, didn't he?
Fletcher killed Carla.

Now, he tells me to go to Harrison's house.
I suppose I'll agree,
Not for me,
But for my safety,
As a notion of my defence crumbles down to sand.
I wrestle my own feelings,
My woes,
Until deep down I understand what this is:
Life or death,
Or better yet, a race against death.

Could I find out who the killer was before being killed?
Was it too late for me?
Was the killer now standing beside me, knocking the door to the other presumed killer's house?
Oh my god!
I'm walking into a trap.

Harrison

Their visit was strange,
Ever so strange.
I look down at myself.

Surely, they have come to turn me in?
But then, as I invite them in,
The door slams shut.
Someone follows us in,
Someone tall, muscular.
A stern facial expression lay on their face.
Him.

The police officer at the scene.

'All are one.'
The lock clicked.
They were stuck in the house,
Until further notice they presumed,
The way the police officer loomed over their faces,
Peering down and doomed.

'Nobody is leaving this room until one confesses;
I know one of *you* did it,
Now who?
This could take seconds or days: what is your pick?'
Silence.

It echoed the room so loudly.

It spoke more words than one,
A drilling pace of one's own face.
Does it kill them inside?
In fact, would they all make it out alive?

'I didn't do it, I swear.'
'You dare.'

Duffy nods.

'I couldn't have.'
'You shouldn't have.'

Fletcher nods.

'I wasn't involved.'
'Then have this solved.'

I nod.

However, I'm not certain;
Everything is a blur,
My eyes begin to hurt,
I bury myself in the dirt,
A spurt of confessions coming my way.
Could it be I that confessed or am I somehow innocent?

My taste is virulent.

Fletcher

What is he thinking?
It wasn't me.
A he, not a she,
A she, not a he.
Who knows?
But it was not me.

I was sleeping all night,
Not thinking about a homicide.
I left Harrison and off he went,
Round the bend,
A knife in his pocket ready to pounce.
I can see it so clearly now,
In a vision,
A word that must ignite,
A sign full of wallowing and ripe.
He did it,
He killed her,
He killed her,
He killed her.

That lying traitor he-

They're staring at me,
Beady eyes menaces of my demise.
Duffy and Harrison,
My friends and enemies,
What are they to me?

Pawns,
Outspoken sinners?
One of them did it, I am telling you.
Now we shall just wait,
Letting the truth eagerly expose itself.

Duffy

One word from me,
Dead.

He's dead,
Done, dusted.
Fletcher or Harrison,
I don't care.
One killed Carla because I sure didn't.
They will pay,
They will pay,
They will pay.

What eager nothing spurred my ears?
I'm cold,
Lifeless,
Afraid.
Nothing makes sense.
I jump to my feet,
Cursed words inside of me.
I hate their guts,
I hate their sighs and their solemn cries, obscured,
Mystical drowns and roars,
The echo inside me,
Parasite light.
The box of secrets opens in front of me.
I'm convinced it's true;
Fletcher did it.

Carla

I can tell you who did it
But what fun would that be?
Even from the grave, having a devious impact.
Of course,
I'm not thrilled I'm dead.
I didn't have much time
But as they fester in me,
My every breath, step, becomes harsh and glacial.
Everything in me is dragged out of proportion
And being at its best becomes too far
Gone.

Although, honestly,
Death isn't too bad;
It's rather peaceful.
Subtly, blood grips the table edge as I slide down,
Underneath, to an abyss, until
All I do,
All I can say, is signs of solitude,
Menaces of the well-hidden,
Trained eye as my hand itches.
Glitches spurt water out of my eye and into my mouth clenching my thirst,
My driven times and hearse.

Do as I say!
He said as he trapped me in his car,
Ready to be taken.

But that's not what happened to me;
I wasn't kidnapped
Or killed by an enemy or stranger.
I was killed by a friend;
Tattooed in my heart it is.
I hate the world,
The one that killed me,
Made me suffer in my head.
How could they?
Shouldn't have!
Wouldn't have!
Couldn't have!

But.
They.
Did.

Harrison

But the two look at me as if I am the one who did this,
As if I am the one who pulled out the knife
And then held it by its bloody handle.

I would never.
I *could* never.

Something tells me the murderer is trying to frame me
But which one is doing it, I ask?
Shielded by a mask,
My task:
Find the killer.

Fletcher

That dirty little liar.

Harrison,
Who stares at me at night,
Lingering, ready to kill outside of daylight.
Poor Carla, unable to resist his wrath as he slaughtered her,
Leaving her in pieces
To die.

He claims he had no involvement;
He's clearly hiding something,
Trying to frame me,
Make me the villain,
The antagonist of this damn story.
No!
I won't have it.
I *will* get what I want.

All I can say is that I am innocent,
Without a doubt;
All you have to do is believe me.

All three of us,
And the officer, of course,
Sit in the locked room for a while in silence.
None of us know what to do
But one of us is guilty and hiding a secret.

They need a confession.
It's not me
Which means the killer is right in front of me.
The question is: who did the brutal murder?
My money is on Harrison,
The story all fits.
Can nobody see it?

I'm a lone wolf ready to cry,
I'm a good guy, a good boy,
Always have been.
Now, I am being accused of a messy situation,
Potentially ruining my reputation,
Tarnishing my life.
I can already imagine the wrongly-placed handcuffs on my hand.
I was practically hanged.
I dig myself deeper into the sand, a hole which I can never escape;
That's the idea:
To escape my wrong accusations.

Duffy

It's tense in the room.
I want so desperately to leave
But I'm locked in beyond a doubt.
I shan't even try running to the door and pulling it at full force.
Two reasons;
One, it's pointless,
Two, it'll only raise suspicion.
I'm in a bad enough place as it is,
Let alone if I mess it up further.

I just can't believe she's dead.

I loved her;
She rejected me but I still longed for her.
I'm devastated with no time to grieve.
I didn't want it to be hands of hatred that held her for the last time;
I wanted it to be loving hands,
Hands of adoration.
Instead,
They were murderous hands.
I might just about kill the two in front of me based on suspicion;
I can't tell who
But one is guilty.
And when I find out,
They *will* pay.

Harrison

I look through the window,
Panting, and my breath slows.
It's clear it's getting to me.
Despite that,
Nobody knows.

The tornado of ideas surrounds me
Like darkness, so cold.
An aching part arouses me.
I'm light as a feather,
Stiff as a board.

They're blaming me for this crime.
I wouldn't dare.
I know it seems like it but I wasn't there,
I swear.

"Are any of you going to confess," the detective says.

I sit and wait.
No one can keep a straight face.
It's a race but no one confesses,
No one dresses for the occasion,
Midnight persuasion.
We've been here for hours now,
Hours of a lonely heart and one big soul,
Just waiting for the final card to be played.
When the battle is lost and won,

The day ends in blood;
Carla Davey died in the flood of melancholy.

"Come on," the detective says. "Just confess."
They oppress their words,
Their fears,
Desires,
Beyond mistresses and heathens.
Nobody answers still.

Just a hard pill to swallow,
Blood stained on the doornail
Like metal painted red.
I wait for you instead,
Under the frame,
Book of distain.
I wander mindlessly till I reach a conclusion;
Duffy did it.
She killed Carla.

She had the motive,
The passion,
The reason:
Unrequited love.
Never forgave,
Letting Carla not be saved.
Murdered with passion in her heart.
Love, from the start, turned murderous.
Love in days turned mischievous.
How could she?

Why would she?

Kill Carla?

Fletcher

A love machine,
A well oiled machine;
I am one, I am all.
I am powerful and strong
But I didn't do this,
I couldn't have.
They can think it,
Be my guest,
But I know deep down
It wasn't me;
It never was.

Something inside of me says it's Harrison,
Stupid Harrison,
With his stuck up attitude and innocent face,
What a disgrace,
I say.
Who did it?
I say.
Who did it?
I disagree,
It wasn't me,
It wasn't me;
It was definitely he.

Duffy

I hate him,
I hate Fletcher.

He did this,
He ripped her heart out and shoved a knife in,
Killing her.
I still don't believe it,
I just have a hunch that it was him,
Him all along,
Him with the dark eyes that linger at night,
Ready to strike.
He did this,
I know it.

Just wait for me and begin,
Thick as thick skin.
Lovingly heard curse
Wanders in from within,
I hear the creak.
Magical sleep,
A court of people;
Where do I begin?
The ripping of skin?

Hate the world,
Loathe the story,
Hitch a ride,
Never survive.

I've been more cautious since Carla's death,
More aware,
Looking and staring without a care,
Loving the red and wonderful air,
A kingdom of great despair,
Looking back on all of the times
As I say goodbye to her loving hands.
Strands of darkness wave and dance,
Prance with a freelance mind of coal,
Stole,
Never old,
Just do as you're told.

Carla

They grabbed me by the wrist one time,
Threatened to kill me.
I didn't take it seriously at the time
But as the moment flashed before my eyes,
A devil in disguise,
I cared not for excuses.
I now know they meant it.
People always say "they're empty threats."
How do you know when they're not?
When they give you a bad feeling,
Make it so you don't sleep at night,
All due to fright.
I know the feeling
And it foreshadowed my death;
One last breath.

Harrison

We look at each other,
Each dead in the eye,
Waiting for a sigh,
One of relief,
Deep, deep misdemeanour.
I see their faces;
They think I am evil,
Cold-hearted sinner.
But what I forget
Is one of these two is innocent,
Wrongly accused,
But which one?
Because I feel bad for them and some.

Duffy

Waiting,
Waiting,
Waiting
For the truth to be exposed,
Cut by the thorn of a rose.
Looking for the type I see,
Begs the question:
Who stands behind me?

I hate my hair,
The way I dress,
The way I hardly impress,
The way that Carla did,
The way she had the whole world hooked,
The way others stopped and looked.

I was one of them.

The moment I met her, I fell in love,
With her looks,
Messy yet perfect hair,
Bold eyes,
Potent smile,
Daring fingernails pattering on my thigh.
I wanted her to be in love,
I was,
I loved her to bits.
But she didn't love me back.

I suppose I can't hate her for it.
I mean, she can't help it.
She's not a lesbian like me,
She's straight,
And though that disheartened me,
I understood.
I don't like boys,
I get it,
I would.

Leave my menace behind
And grievances to another kind.
I still love her,
Her laugh,
Her smile,
The way she winked and left.
I love it all.
Shame she didn't feel the same way about me.

Carla

I left,
I fled,
Nothing left,
In the scene,
A scenario,
A dream.
Within me, I scream;
He's chasing me.
I dart,
Nothing left in me to run.
He pins me down,
Turns me around,
My head on the concrete.
But nobody hears my cries,
My solemn goodbyes.
But I didn't die that day,
I escaped intact,
Cracked but hardly back.
I survived,
I survived,
I survived!

Fletcher

I hate the day she died,
I hate the way the other two lied,
I hate it, I hate it, I hate it.
I hate the time and crime,
Until I said goodbye.

It's devastating news,
Provoking the blues,
Until I leave the lie, saying goodbye.

"Be honest with me Fletcher, did you kill her?"
Harrison asks.
I didn't,
How dare he ask?
How dare he suspect?
How dare he live in manacles that live and protect?
I'll do it until I leave my regret.

Sing the ruins,
Sing until I hum,
Till the work is forever done.
I roar in rage,
I sing my praise,
I answer "No."

Duffy

Upset, I regret my love.
Fletcher's denying all involvement;
I don't know if I buy it.
How he can deny it
So easily.
I mean,
Motive?
Passion?
Killer?
He has it all;
Will he admit it?
I don't know.
Just let it snow.

Harrison

Dying for a cause,
I'd have died for Carla,
Her sweet personality,
Loving gaze,
Smiley personality.
She was a beautiful person.

I look at the others,
Guilty as charged.
They aren't innocent by any means
But one is better than the other;
I just can't put my finger on who.

Each person becomes evermore suspicious as time ticks on,
Likely business and unlikely innocence,
Time becomes one and one becomes time,
Everything shudders.
They become more guilty to me the longer I stare.
I hardly care for them,
Only for Carla
Of whom I speak,
Making things so bleak.

Frail and rambunctious times and tales,
Looking into rare sightings,
Sales of blood,
Of gore.

What do they have in store?
I hate the way they lie,
Cry, say it like it's devastating when it's not.
Tie the knot into two,
I'll always love you.

Fletcher

Cry tears of joy,
That's what I'd do if they gave up questioning me,
Questioning us.
What we do,
What we say,
Don't let them get away.

I want the killer to be locked away,
In ghost chains ripping at their soul,
Tugging it in hell.
They deserve it,
I know they do,
I am well aware.
The solace of incessant screaming tells me so,
Let her go, let her go!

That poor girl,
Poor Carla,
As blood pours out of her vessel,
Losing everything,
Her life, and everything that came with it.
Uncalled for,
Underserved.
Who could be so evil to do such a thing?

Let's wait for a confession.

Carla

In my dreams,
I am suspended in the air,
Flying down,
Looking on the works of many,
Buildings, all the things I didn't get to see because I died.
Dead.
Dust of the past.

Wondering what it's like to be alive,
Be the person I wish I was,
One that survived.

I recount that day so well.
I'm all alone, by my side on my phone.
Suddenly, a loud noise.
I shake, drop the phone.
Though,
Before I could pick it up,
I'm stabbed,
Right in the back.
When I say it went right through me,
I mean it,
As it shattered my flesh barrier and went straight for my organs.

They sprint.

I'd turned around and just about got a glimpse of them
Before I fell to the ground,
Unable to stand any longer,
Unable to move,
Unable to do most things.
Blood poured out of me like a spilt jug.
I didn't bother trying to clean it up;
What difference would it have made?
I'd be dead in minutes.

Nobody sees me
And if they did,
They were too scared or didn't care,
As I died in front of my own eyes,
As I looked down
And watched the blood trickle down my stomach,
All alone and betrayed.

A friend turned foe,
Oh, I had loved them so.

Duffy

'Hate the game, not the player,' they say.
I say, 'hate the player.'
Yes, they didn't make the rules
But they made the decision.
The rules;
They can be stupid.
I don't understand,
It wasn't the plan,
I would have ran.

Then, we speak.

"Where were you the day Carla was killed?" the officer asked me.
I grasped my story and told it him straight,
"I didn't kill her, this must be a mistake."

Leading the path I chose on,
I tell the story,
I tell it well,
Until the end comes
And I know the response all too well.

Things are becoming more and more tense,
Defence of the heart,
Defence of the mind,
I hate the time that I am behind.

Its hatred is upsetting,
Like time and bind,
Lies are gone,
Just a creative shoulder,
Looking at me from behind
Like evil in mankind.
The devil, too bad, too mad.

Wait, just yet,
The battle of guilt is just beginning,
Rotten imaginings,
Tainted scars,
Reaching the world from afar.

Who actually did it, and, most importantly, why?

Fletcher

Carla was a mysterious woman,
Left quite a bit to the imagination,
To the mind.
One of a kind she was,
Until she left our world and became another statistic,
A dream,
A courteous one of a kind being,
One, all, together.

I wanted her,
To be her partner.
She rejected me,
Rejected the idea of us.
I wanted to hold her till the end,
Till dawn became dusk,
Her partner in crime.
It was all good until that moment,
The time when good said bad and bad said good.

She was good,
Till she was bad.

Harrison

Tugging on the wall,
Almost ethereal,
My bones break,
My hands numb,
All I can think of was how I knew she was the one.

"On the night I was all alone,
Reading a book in the quietude of my room,
Not at all involved in doom," I say.

"But you were drunk, how can you say,
Something may have gotten in the way?"
The officer said, full of dread.

Something is untimely ruined,
Ripped, never slipped,
Dipped in a courteous sound,
Never found,
Doomed to a world of wonder,
All a cluster.

How do I know what to say,
When a sick sense of fear,
Evermore, gets in the way?

So I leap,
The drip down the wonderful grounds of what was
solemnly found.

I hate the day he got in the way
Of a murderous glee that never occurred,
Never learned,
Never turned.

Duffy

She was my world.

Everything I did was for her,
All for her,
All for her mind, her smile,
Daylight for a while.
Thunder wakes me up at night,
In spite of the roads that take me.
I spare,
Rarities just laugh at me.
I create a magnificent charm
But am in nobody's arms
But her's who rejected having mine.

She was sweet about it, I guess.
Nothing in the world ever made sense,
I was gone,
Alone,
Figment of one's imagination.
And I am thrown
By the darkest depths of the night;
I shriek and shudder,
I just might..

Carla

I'm a dead girl.

Nobody seems to truly care about me,
Only about the dead body.
Not the dead girl,
The soul, drifting off,
Ready to be saved,
Ready for a good day;
One that never came.

I'm lost.
I don't know where I belong
And all I can hear is the echo of arguing,
About me,
About who did it.
I know who did it,
I know who did it.
But they can't hear me;
I'm just a solemn ghost.

Lurking, a host.

Fletcher

I sit in the room.
It's beginning to get cold
And dark.
The officer stares at me;
What the hell have I ever done wrong?
Maybe my toleration level is low,
My temper a little too high?
But I am not a killer,
Am I?

Just wait for the day where I can get away,
Settle for dismay,
Waiting for the crowd
To cheer and say hooray.

I want to be a hero,
A person people look up to.
What am I if not?
A loner?
A loser?

I don't want to be that.
I want to be strong and powerful,
Anger on my side,
Hiding a goodbye.
I want to be the one that wears the hat and says good day.
I need to flee,

Get away.

Duffy

"Admit it, one of you," Fletcher says.
I spit, I didn't do it,
Maybe *he* did.
Is he trying to frame us for his mistake or was it
Harrison all along?
Waiting for a bullet to pierce my skin,
The battle will soon begin
As I slide my hand down my thigh and pull out a pen
and a piece of scrap paper.
Then, I say,
"Write on it."

They say, "What?"
I say, "Write on it."
They say, "Write what?"
"What you were doing," I say;
I shan't let them get away,
Never,
Not my damned endeavour.
I'm innocent in all of this.
Please just leave me out.
I'm built for help not lies,
Not cries.
As flies flutter around me like a storm,
I am informed:
New evidence has come to light.
So my body,
Eagerly,

Takes flight.

Harrison

One.

Two.

Three.

Four.

Five.

Six.

Seven.

Eight.

Nine.

Ten.

Here we go again.

The same questions,
The same stupid answers.

Somebody clearly has their story straight.
We may never know
Who awoke and chose Carla to kill that dreary day.

She took my breath away.

Will we be stuck in this room forever?
My mind wonders as I linger through shadow and bone,
One world a home for the wicked,
One for the good.

I am neither, I am both, I am one.

Carla

Fletcher, Harrison or Duffy?

Who do you think did it?

I suppose the detective will find that out.

Won't he?

Blood slipped away from my body as I died.
I knew it oh so well as my lungs gave in.
I passed away, into the abyss.

Now I am a ghost in the darkness,
Waiting for my applause.

Who is so sweet yet so harsh to know?

Fletcher

Just a smiley face on a guilty girl.
After much consideration,
I think it's Duffy,
With her potent smirk and long hair of secrets.
Harrison, he just *seemed* guilty,
But I am betting on Duffy,
Guilty as charged.

"I'm waiting for you to confess," the officer says.
I just wait,
"It wasn't me,"
I say.
It couldn't have been,
It wouldn't have been.
Murdered?

I never expected
But what actually happened that night,
Was it traumatic?
Harsh?
Dark?
Or plain evil?
Let's find out..

Duffy

"Did either of you do it?" I scream.
Just a dream,
I'm mad.
We've been here for almost twenty-four tedious hours,
Watching the clock tick.
I'm in a circle of terror,
Sitting across from a murderer.
One should confess.
The longer we sit there,
The more I hate them,
The lying sinners,
The seemingly superior.
It chills my bones to the core;
Who would want to kill poor Carla,
An innocent?

"Just admit it," I yell.
They could tell
I was sad,
Mad
And a tad disconsolate.
I open the gate to heaven;
I'm confident of my innocence,
I know I'll enter.
But will Fletcher or Harrison?
That is the question
Determined by who of the two shed blood.

"Just tell me," I scream once again.
Silence.
"Tell me," I scream.
Silence.
Rude silence,
Tense silence,
Emotional silence.

I don't want to listen to the nonsense they preach anymore.
I want the truth.
I want answers.

Harrison

Duffy is mad,
Sad,
Angry,
Cranky.

She's hating the world,
The balance of nature,
I understand.

But I also know
I didn't do this.

She doesn't actually seem guilty
Which leaves Fletcher;
He very much keeps to himself,
No doubt.
Can I crack his shell and make him speak?
We'll see,
We'll see.

Fletcher

I am a shadow of the man I once was,
Consumed by fear,
Fear of the murderer,
Fear for my sanity,
My love,
Gone,
Taken by the storm of sin,
A storm of evil,
One of no return,
Once solemn.
I don't know what to do without you.
You, Carla,
You were everything...

Residing in those eyes was a light that never dimmed,
Until her day of death I suppose.
God forbid I admit I am scared,
I've been through hell and back at this point,
Wanting answers for Carla's death,
Knowing the murderer is sat in front of me,
Right now.

I ask, "Which one of you is telling absolute lies?"
I want to swear
But I think, in front of the officer, it would give the wrong impression
So I keep my cool the best I can.
But neither of them answers,

Neither of them does.
And at this point we are getting nowhere
So the officer decides to take the situation into his own hands,
Hands more capable…

Duffy

Fletcher's mad.
The officer has left the room,
Everything is falling to pieces,
Steadily but surely.
Fletcher has the nerve to call me the sinner!
The longer this goes on,
The more and more convinced I am that it's, *guess who?*
Fletcher!

That menace of a man,
The killer.
Harrison may be a little off
But I doubt he's the killer.
I would be surprised raw
And, if it's me,
Well, I wouldn't have known.

Part with my body,
I'd give my life to see the truth,
See what you don't see,
Until the officer says, "Listen to me."

Harrison

"This is going far too slow," the officer says.
"Let's speed it up so we can all go," the officer exclaims.
Panting at my own pace,
Just wanting to escape.
But I can't;
I am trapped in here until someone admits.

I think Duffy is the killer.
I have some doubt
But at the moment,
Her innocent little act isn't fooling me;
Her confidence,
Her rejection from Carla,
She has motive,
Passion,
What more do I need to say?

Fletcher seems to think I'm the killer,
I can tell,
But where is my motive compared to Duffy's?
Where is my passion?
Invisible because it doesn't exist.
Now, the officer begins to get mad;
He's yelling.
I block it all out,
Until he says, "No doubt one of you did this, now who here is the selfish one?"

I mean,
I can't argue;
He's preaching the truth.
I just want out of here,
Justice too.

Fletcher

Wherever I am, I think of Carla
But this officer is shouting at us like hell.
I mean,
It's a bit far,
We know.
I assume it's Harrison,
With his, 'oh woe is me' attitude.
The sun is not mine,
The moon is not his,
The light is Carla's.
Harrison now looks teary-eyed;
Breaking through him is clearly a sinister guilt.
I'm waiting for him to confess;
Will it happen?

Duffy

Oh tortured soul,
Save him.
Harrison is a wreck;
He balls his eyes out.
Now, it's twilight
And the darkness outside reflects his manner.
Just let him free from the devil's latch,
Pull him close and love him.
But then, something happens,
Something I didn't expect.

"I did it," Harrison says. "I killed Carla."

Harrison

What did I just do?
I was sick, tired, worn-down;
I wanted out.
But I just admitted to murder
And, well, I didn't do it.
Now there's no going back.

Damn, I made a mistake;
A killer's going to be lose,
I'll be locked up for life,
Carla won't have justice,
Not true justice,
No, no, no!
What have I done?
I've messed up so bad
But I suppose nobody will believe me now,
Not after I allegedly confessed in front of an officer.
I mean,
I'm screwed.
I'm screwed forever.
What am I to do?

Fletcher

He confessed, he confessed!
We're out of here,
Free,
Glee!
I could lose my arms in Duffy's in excitement but she pulls away;
She still seems suspicious.
But what about?
Harrison confessed;
What more evidence do you need?
She's not satisfied, I guess.
This whole things is a mess
As I dress up in my mourning black.
Less is more,
What is in store?
Dust?

I let myself get too close to a life's imprisonment.
Looking back,
I probably acted poorly.
But I am better now;
Now I can allow a better future,
A better me. In a letter,
I will write to Harrison,
Saying he deserved whatever he got.

Duffy

He confessed;
I know it's Fletcher,
I know it.
It can't be-
It shan't be,
Harrison he,
He's just broken,
Not a manipulative sinner.
There must be some explanation:
He lied to get out?
He wanted to save me?
He did it without thinking?
Surely, it's one.

I need to prove his innocence,
I must.
But, as my heart clenches,
Handcuffs are placed on Harrison as he is dragged away.
I squeal inside,
Not from excitement,
But anxiety and pressure.
It's all on me now
To get justice,
Get Harrison's freedom.

Save everyone.

Harrison

I can't believe I am handcuffed,
A new chapter of my life,
One in bars.
There is still the court case
But since I confessed,
I'm guessing there will be little debate.
My future is fractured,
My sanity,
My innocence,
All at once.
Oh, what have I done?
What have I done?

Carla

My death is ripping lives apart.
Doing more damage than needed.
I know who did this
And for goodness sake they have it all wrong.
They have the wrong person.
All I can do is sigh,
Goodbye for now,
Goodbye their time.

Fletcher

Finally,
They're locked up for good, I guess.
Luck?
I think not,
Pure guilt?
Yes.

I knew they'd find me innocent in the end,
I knew from the start I was fine,
Just a sign of my clean hands,
Never once touching blood.
I can walk away knowing I'll never stay
In a cell that takes my time away.
It's not yet over for me
But it is for him,
All because he stupidly sinned.

Duffy

Fletcher, guilty, not charged,
I say,
Detective Duffy on the way.
Oh, that's cringy,
But it's okay.
I suppose it'll never hear or see the light of day.
I must take matters into my own hands,
Make my own plans;
From the doors of ruin,
I paint a new picture.
Once of blamelessness and one of blame,
One of bloody hands, stained forever,
And one of hands forever clean,
The only blood they've seen is wounds of their own,
Scratches,
Cuts.
All those falls
That makes what you call melancholy memories of tears.

Years go by;
It feels like years
But it's been only hours.
As I return home and map out my evidence,
It's here,
I'm here.
I will have proof
And, when I am ready,

I'll release incriminating evidence to the world.

Harrison

In my dreams,
I'm banging on the bars of the cell yelling,
"Let me out, let me out."
But I can't,
I certainly shan't.
Likely, it would, in their eyes,
Incriminate me more.
So I sit on my bed,
Rotten as it is,
Unable to sleep,
Breathe or eat.
They think it's guilt;
I think it's anxiety's feast.

At least I have time alone,
Not questioned now.
People have their answers,
As many as I can give.
But what they don't have is the killer
Or what happened to Carla Davey.
That, I truly don't know.
I couldn't tell you,
Only mere details shown of the news.
What am I even to say when the trial comes?
Do I just let the killer get away?
I think not.

Now, at this point,

I have nothing to lose.
By my own statement,
I have already lost it all:
My life,
My future,
My reputation,
All gone.

So fight me, you raging beast of a killer,
I have nothing left to lose.
All I can do now
Is gain.

Fletcher

I can just imagine Harrison locked up now,
Stationary in guilt,
Still trying rapidly
To wash the blood of his hands that plague him and night.
Whilst I take flight,
In a storm so big,
So loud,
It takes my breath away.

Duffy

On my wall now resides a board,
Typical, like in the movies,
Of string, pictures and sticky notes,
All nicely colour coordinated like so.

I'm fighting for the right cause,
I'm sure,
More than sure,
Certain,
Certain enough to be doing this,
Using my time,
Reputation,
To fight for Carla,
Fight for Harrison,
Gain karma for Fletcher,
Leave the world as is,
Let the darkness in and close the box.
The whole world blatantly rocks.
I close the door as my bedroom shakes.
Never are there earthquakes;
Am I going crazy?
Is this a dream?
I wake up,
My heart in a stutter
In a world of pain.
I mutter, "What happens next?"

Harrison

Turning the tables around,
I have changed my mind.
Of course,
I always thought the killer was Duffy
But now I am not so sure.
The light Fletcher shines in seems dark, dull and evil.
Seeing black dreariness and that only,
I realise something unholy.

Fletcher killed Carla in revenge.
My fists are so tense,
Rejection the piece of the puzzle everyone needs.
I could punch the hell out of him;
Where is he?
Get me out now!

Fletcher

The clock ticks,
Never hits.
The killer locked away,
All I can say is hooray.
Thank you for everything,
The revenge;
It feels so sweet,
Like ice
Scraping against my feet.
Oh. deadly sins,
Fright my hair,
Strands stay up; just a harness from above.
I never speak,
I never listen,
I just watched the story unfold.

Duffy

Tracking every responsibility,
Taking every responsibility,
As it all goes down in flames.

I am no stranger from bloody skies.
I wake up alone,
Always afraid I'll need to run,
Sprint for my survival.
Everything exits my body as I collapse to the ground,
Scared I believe he is the one.
But for Carla,
I'd let the world go up in a blaze
So I shall do whatever it takes.

Some may call me a stalker for what I do next,
I call it bravery.

I follow Fletcher's every move,
With my camera and notebook, of course,
Photographing and recording anything suspicious,
Anything incriminating.
For days,
Nothing.

Until one day,
He returns from the shop with a ton of bleach and gloves.
Now, he could just be cleaning

Or is he washing away any evidence he could still have remaining
In case he is ever questioned again?

I snap a picture and duck down behind the bush,
Then look back up again.
In his car, placed there recently,
Is a large mysterious box.

I have this gut feeling
So, as he gets in his car,
I get in mine.
I begin to tail him,
Down the road,
Following his eerie, every move
To a dumping sight.
He leaves the car for a second;
The car boot is still open.

Here is my opportunity.
I open the box;
I find a blood stained knife,
Cut-up, shredded blood stained clothes and shoes,
All thoroughly bleached.
I wanted to take it there and then
But that would ruin my chances.
So I snap a picture and run back to my car as Fletcher returns,
Confident and all.
Him, entirely ignorant to what I just did,
Exposed.

I was right;
I knew Harrsion was innocent,
I knew it.
The officer has been so blind;
Lets just hope the jury isn't.

Harrison

I'm stuck,
Likely forever.
I don't know what is going on outside of here.
All I know
Is that I am still in this cell,
The killer still roams free,
The whole situation is messed up.
I'm telling you,
This needs to end.

I just don't know how it can.

Fletcher

I'll admit it:
I've been lying.

I killed Carla,
I did it
And it felt so good.
The power, the passion, the control;
I've never felt so alive.
But the aftermath is the hard part;
How to get away with murder?
So far,
I've done a good job.
Never did I bet one of them would confess
But wow did it make my job easier.

I felt such a rush;
It's so desirable,
So sickeningly desirable.
I crushed her.
I loved her.
She rejected me.
She got what she deserved and more.

Damned you spirit,
Take me to hell,
Take me to hell.
It's more a reward to be around evil than good;
I have no regrets.

Duffy

I continue to follow him,
Watch over Fletcher like a hawk.
Manacles of distress linger around my hands,
Fear in my eyes.
If he finds out,
Am I as good as dead?
Am I his property forever?
Oh, please surrender me from such a fate.
I trust nobody now.
Carla trusted Fletcher
And look what he did.
How am I supposed to see past that?
I have no idea,
Just watch and wait
Till I open the gate to hell
And push him inside.

I am hovering beside his house,
Just watching and waiting for more evidence to occur.
When I doubt my decision,
I think of Carla.
I'm doing this for Carla,
My love, my everything,
Though she didn't feel the same.
I just feel a golden spree of midnight howls.
I can't run,
I cannot hide;
Fletcher has caught me.

I am done,
Gone.
Likely dead.

So he pins me down,
He says, "What are you doing here?"
I stutter my response quickly,
The best I can,
Lost in the fog of my brain,
Though there is still further to fall.
"Bird watching," I say.
"I don't buy it," he replies.
Darn it, I've lost,
He's going to kill me,
He's going to kill me,
But I am not dead yet.
"Speak a word of this, you're dead as a doornail,"
Fletcher says.

He leaves.

I'm scared to death;
He cost my mind,
My sanity.
I want to leave,
Frightfully sprint away.
I can't;
I have everything to lose.

Harrison

The trial is fast approaching;
I don't know what to do.
My body is aching,
My hands are stuttering in form;
What am I to do?
They all see me as a guilty killer
But that's not me.
That's not what I see.
But what does that matter?
The main opinion is the world
And I doubt they see me for me.
I'll be dead inside soon,
Dead, goodbye.

Fletcher

I still can't believe I got away with it.
Murder?
Really?
But Duffy is on my trail,
I must prevail.
Nobody will believe that spiteful girl over me,
Surely?
But as my breath slows
And I start panting,
I realise there is only one logical thing to do;
Kill her *too*.

But who do I frame it on?
Or should Duffy just disappear?

Duffy

Who knew things would get so crazy?
My friend,
My love,
Killed.
Harrison, falsely imprisoned,
My life is on the line.

Could this get much worse?
I doubt so.
Every day I have alive is more and more anxiety-
provoking;
I know my time is ticking away the closer we get to
the trial.
My world is crashing down.
I don't know how
But I know why.

Yet, despite my better judgement,
I continue to secretly follow Fletcher.
But now,
Even further under the radar,
Like a sorrowful bliss,
Never missed.

I pack my bags of evidence,
Take it to the police.
They don't believe me;
They think this is all formed by raging angst.

It's not.

It's me and my demon coming out to say:
You can't hide anymore;
I'll begin to let you decay.

I leave the station in tears,
My life even more at risk.
Nobody believes me;
What am I to do?
Who knew?
All I know is that the trial is my golden opportunity.
As long as I stay alive till then,
I remain relatively intact,
Until it lacks.

Harrison

Three days remain until my trial now.
My heart is beating like a drum,
My brain running so fast I cannot speak.
Outsiders would think me weak;
I suppose I am,
Confessing to a murder I never committed,
Confessing to a crime never entirely solved.
Even I beg the question,
Why?

I feel so vulnerable right now,
I cry myself to sleep every night,
Pray for release in the daylight.
I'm sad for a multitude of reasons
But mostly for Carla;
What if she doesn't get the justice she deserves?
What does that make her?
What does that make me?
I may just as bad at the one who stabbed her,
Just as cruel as led her lifeless body to an even worse fate;
One of lies.

I look into my own eyes,
Letting the sinner's valour rise,
There lies a body of misfits and mediocre dungeons,
Visits from the devil,
Stooping down to my idiotic level.

I lay,
Wanting to stay,
Wanting to go.
Oh, who knows?

Fletcher

I could kill Duffy,
Threaten her future with my knife.
I've done it before,
I'd do it again
And again
And again
Until my heart breaks to solace.
My mind patterns against the window of blood drips,
Not rain droplets but bloody stains,
Causing red to stain as it evaporates upwards,
Chucking my brain into mush.
I feel a rush.
How I long for that addictive murder feeling again.
It's like a hobby,
My comfort,
And who better than Duffy,
To shut her up,
Make her quiet.
Let me live my life in peace!
She'll never seize to exist,
I tell you.
The day is too cruel to let her.
I, Fletcher, am too cruel.

Duffy

Blood runs down the wall of names,
I hear you.
Fear's a painted devil.
I look upon my achievements with a sense of despair,
I long for something I once knew true,
Love.

Three days to the trial.
What do I have?

Pictures,
Video,
Noted-down incidents.
Hopefully with a compelling story it's enough.
I just need to put myself forward
As a witness.

Harrison

Two days to my trial;
What can I do?
Get my story straight.
Motive?
Hardly solid.
Who else would have done it?
Fletcher Mcarthy,
A ambiguous man,
Full of secrets,
Hopefully someone behind the scenes.
Somehow knows;
Let the truth be exposed.

Carla

He killed me, he killed me!
I can never forgive him.
I constantly ask myself, why?
Why he didn't allow me to say goodbye?
It's just cruelty.
My emotions are naked,
My wrist scratched.
I want to be free;
Please,
Get justice at last.

Fletcher

Kingdoms bow to me.
Where my demons hide,
It's dark inside.
I am called by Satan's mist,
God's fury,
For the mess I made;
One congratulations, one of loathing.

I dare you,
Get too close to me,
Meet a sticky end,
Pen and paper in hand,
The knife lingers in my hand
Around the bend.
Let me pack a bag
Of killing supplies;
I am ready to kill Duffy.
It's time.

Duffy

Two days till trial
And I'm scared for my life,
Never thinking,
Never looking back.
I am building up fear that may never go away,
A paranoia far from okay.
I need help
But they'd see my crazy.
My whole life is a shambles.
I still need you Carla,
I still need to take your hand.
Why did you leave me?
Why did you leave me
Helpless?
Chills in my bones,
I scream.
I still need you Carla.
I hate you Fletcher.

Harrison

I just want to go home,
Be saved from the madness.
This cell of defeat,
I am getting depressed,
I'm getting crazy.
My mind in flames,
My hands burning off,
All I see is my face and smeared blood on the mirror.

They aren't calling me royalty;
They are calling me dead.

Fletcher

I'm cruel.
I know that.

Will I ever learn?
How do I linger around knowing what I did?
I'm too excited,
I want to shout it out.
But damn the world.
I can't,
I'd be locked up
Forever.

The trial is tomorrow
And, if I am being completely honest here,
I am a nervous wreck,
What if Duffy spills the truth
Or new evidence comes to light?
I need a clean sweep,
Is that too much to ask?

Duffy

One day to trial.
I am a mess.

I feel so unprepared
And there is a funny thing in my throat,
Asking me what and why I care.
It's life or death.
Fletcher gets put away?
Justice is served.
Harrison free?
I am safe.
He walks away?
Harrison trapped,
No justice for Carla,
I am as good as dead.

There is a lot of pressure and people don't even know it.
Just wait for the bell to ring.
I am there.
Hours tick away.
I get ready in my full black dress for the court case,
The trial,
Wondering,
What happens next?

Harrison

I hate the way Fletcher lies
And what becomes of Duffy.
Is she in danger?

We are one hour away from the trial,
My life, just fading steadily away,
Like a time bomb.
I hope someone puts a stop to it,
Someone today.
If Fletcher gets away,
A murderer is loose.
A man got away with a crime so despicable,
He should be loathed for all eternity.

My breathing suddenly becomes shallow;
I am crying.
I'm on the floor.
I feel paralysed in fear;
It's a panic attack.
I started having them since my time in jail
But none this bad;
The pressure is getting to me.
Oh how pathetically sad.
I lean forth for water
But none is left in the cup.
I feel faint.
My heart beats a million miles an hour
And that's all I remember

As I wake up on the floor.
One minute from the trial.
Here goes everything, I think to myself,
It's all
Or nothing.

Fletcher

I rock up to the trial,
Black suit,
A tie.
I look fine as hell.
Things are just beginning,
I know that well.
But, through the corner of my eye,
I see Duffy Gonner,
A clean smirk on her face.
What a disgrace.
So, I approach her,
My fists red.

Duffy

I am walking down the eerie corridor,
Lurking by me,
Fletcher.

I'm wearing my potent smirk on my face,
Full of glee to take him down.
All is going well until
Suddenly,
Fletcher storms towards me,
Pushing me into a nook and cranny where nobody can see us.

I am pinned against the wall.
I swallow my saliva.
His hand grabbing my wrist,
He says, "Speak a word of this and you're a dead girl."

I hate to admit it
But I am scared.
He's done it before,
He could do it again.
Then his kisses my cheek and says,
"Just sit there and look pretty, won't you?"
And he walks away.

The nerve.

Fletcher

If Duffy speaks,
I swear I'll kill her,
Slowly,
Painfully,
Torturously.
Even one word out of her little mouth
And she's dead.

The knife is already in my pocket,
Just in case.
Even if I go to prison,
At least I'll have my revenge,
My one last taste of my addiction.
I'd leave life with no regrets,
None at all.
My only regret, if she spoke,
Would have been not killing her.

Duffy

I take my seat,
Right at the front,
Paper in my hand;
Guidance on what to say.
I feel extremely nauseous,
Like I'm going to throw up.
But I can't.
Keep your cool, Duffy,
Keep it now.
Things aren't fair,
Things are foul,
Unless you preach what you dare.

Harrison

I enter the courtroom,
Handcuffed in my neon orange jumpsuit,
People staring at me as if I am the embodiment of evil.
Little do they know I am innocent.
It'll be okay,
I tell myself,
It'll be okay.

Duffy

I'm anxious as hell,
Just a mess of something worth nothing.
I trust nobody now,
Not even myself.
I've sunk so deep I may never recover.
Maybe death might not be so bad.
I leap, so dreadfully deep.
I fall under the cracks.
Look what I have become.
I can no longer run,
I can no longer hide;
I may as well risk everything:
My life.

The trial begins.

"You may be seated,"
They say.
I hope, in dismay, the trial will have the right conclusion.
Then they ask,
"Harrison Vangero, do you plead guilty or not guilty
To the murder of Carla Davey?"
"Not guilty," he replies.
I nod.
He is correct.
But I hear whispers all around me;
They think he is a liar,

A cheat.
I know they are wrong
But will the jurors know like me?

Harrison

"Do you know Carla Davey?" they say.
"Yes," I respond.
My legs are shaking,
My teeth
Chattering.
The echoing sound of violent whispers aches me from afar,
Just the scars on my arms of my self-inflicted cuts.
I can almost hear dramatic music play in my head.
Day by day,
A severed thread.
"How do you know Carla Davey?" they ask.
"She was my friend, a- a good friend," I respond.
Tears in my red eyes
As people roll their own.
I can tell my audience is stubborn;
They don't believe me.

"If you are pleading not guilty, may I ask,
Why did you confess?" they say.
"Stress," I say. "I had emotions to express."
"And you were drunk that night, were you not?" they say.
"I was, I remember very little
But little to none of the evidence points to m-"
I say before interruption.
"That is all," they say,
Marching away.

Fletcher

It's all going according to plan.
Of course,
It would have been so much easier had Harrison
pleaded guilty
But no bother;
That was unlikely.
Nobody but damn Duffy believes him anyway.
No one even suspects me;
I'm a poor, innocent victim.
Nobody hurts more than I.
Sigh.
I am just a man
With a plan,
Ready to do whatever it takes.

Even if that means killing once more.

Duffy

I am anxiously awaiting for my moment to take the stand
As a witness;
I am to present evidence,
Unseen before.

"Duffy Gonner to take the stand, please," they say.
Fletcher's grin suddenly fades into one of vexation
As I look upon the audience in terror.
I feel cold,
Mildly numb.
Nothing left to say is done.
It can only go up from here,
I tell myself,
Because you've already accepted death as your friend.

"I stand before you today," I say,
"With evidence not against Harrison but another."
The audience gasp.
I clasp my hands.
I present my pictures, videos,
My account of events,
Collected and collaged in a diary,
And our time with the officer,
In the hope that it would all link up
And show guilt.

Now both Harrison and Fletcher are on trial, together,
As one.
One will leave,
One will stay.
As Fletcher pleads,
"Not guilty," he says.

I rest my case.

Harrison

I knew somebody was fighting for me
Behind the scenes:
Duffy,
You star.
I see you from afar;
Thank you so much,
Thanks a bunch.
But will she face them and be right?
Or will they seek an eager flight and place me in jail?
It's easier,
I confess.
Yes, I pleaded not guilty
But that doesn't rest my case as innocent.
In their eyes, I still did wrong.
Nobody believed me and that stung.
I knew from that moment,
I could be done.

Fletcher

I'm going to kill that girl!
How dare she deceive me?
How dare she look me in the eye
With that smirk in her smile and lie?
She's as good as dead;
She won't ever again sleep in bed.
Now I'm on trial,
Great.
Let's just hope the jury buys none of this
Or so I hope,
So I wish,
So I *need*.

Duffy

I presented my evidence;
I feel better.
But having Fletcher in the room,
For me,
Makes it all the more tense,
All the more chilling
And dreary,
Like the thunder and lighting personified.
I hate it.

The trial went back and forth for hours on end;
I blanked out most of it,
I don't know what was said.
I awoke at the minute the jury came back.
I had sat in that courtroom the whole time during the hour they deliberated;
This was the moment,
The moment I had been waiting for.

"Harrison is not guilty of the murder of Carla Davey," they say
As I let out a huge sigh.
"Fletcher *is* guilty of physical and verbal harassment
And the first degree murder of Carla Davey," they exclaim.
Fletcher drops to the floor.
It is over;
I will survive.

He can't get to me now.

Justice is there for Carla,
Justice for all,
It is because of me;
I can rest now.
I'll be fine,
I'll be fine.

Carla

The story is over,
Justice was served.
Duffy is safe,
Harrison free,
Fletcher where he belongs.
And then there's me,
All alone,
Moving on up to a better place.
My business finished,
All I need to do now
Is wait;
I'm waiting.

A race against death,
Oh how brilliant of a tale.
One of dismay,
One of panic,
One so frail.
I feel it lying there,
All alone.
I feel loved,
Cherished,
That people would sacrifice that much for me;
I just want them to be free.

Free to fly,
Free to be fine,
Free friends and family of mine.

Move on,
See the light,
See what life can bring.
I'd had enough,
It was my turn to go.
Though, too soon;
Guess it wasn't meant to be,
Meant to be there,
Meant to be me.
Fletcher,
Oh, damned he.
He can rot,
Become dust;
I wouldn't care.
But Duffy,
Who I loved as a friend,
Never let go,
Never amend.
It's time to fly,
Say goodbye,
It's a good day.

It's a race against time,
A race that is mine.

About The Author

Hi! My name is Alicia Blossom Lloyd. I am 16 years old and raised in the UK. I wrote my first unpublished book at age 12 and this book at the age of 16.

Writing from a young age has always been my number one passion, even if I didn't realise it. I am an avid reader and especially authors such as Charles Dickens have always inspired me with their impactful works; I strive to do the same, even if it's merely by bringing joy to an otherwise dreary morning.

This is my second book after my debut novel *Murder Board* which is my pride and joy. But this book, *A Race Against Death*, is different for me. As a verse fiction piece, a beautiful form of writing in my opinion and accessible to most, I thoroughly enjoyed writing it due to being a different change of pace.

So if you think "I am too young" or "Too old", ignore it; anyone can write if they put their mind to it and let their imagination thrive as it should. Because, at least for me, I am driven crazy without my words of expression.

I hope you enjoyed my novel and I hope to publish more!

Acknowledgements

I just want to thank some people who have had an impact on my work.

Thank you to my supportive little sister who has always stuck with me through thick and thin, my parents who have assisted me with this endeavour and my close friends who have always pushed me with such enthusiasm.

I would also like to thank my teachers from an early age, infant to my secondary teachers, who have aided in developing my skill, my confidence, my morals and myself as well. I also send my thanks to my past SEND teachers and school librarian who have always made space for me when I was struggling (the school librarian especially as she has always pushed me to keep going, despite setbacks and rejections).

I would also like to thank one of my best friends who selflessly designed this book cover as well as my editor, Faith Fawcett, who helped me to develop this version into what it is today.

I would also like to thank my great, though small, social media community who have helped me to make this what it is today! I am so grateful to these people and just wanted to express that.

Instagram: @aliciablloyd
TikTok: @_alicialloyd
Youtube: @-AliciaLloyd

Printed in Great Britain
by Amazon